I0739210

ALSO BY GREGY ALEXANDER

Deceptive Tales

The Loyalist

The husband who never loved

Gregy Alexander

The husband who never loved. Copyright 2015 by Brian First Publishing. All rights reserved. Any characters, names and places depicted in the story are the works of fiction. And does not reflects on real events or any living persons rather the imagination of the author. In any cases thereof, it's mere coincidental. The following has been copyrighted for the giving rights purposes and is the property of its respective owners and should not be reproduced nor distributed without the written consent of each parties. For more information please visit: brianfirstpub.com

Brian First Publishing books may be purchased for educational, business, or sales promotional use. For information please email BrianFirstPub@gmail.com

Designer - Edward Williams of Money Design, LLC

Editor - Lekha Keister

ISBN: 97809916299091095

ACKNOWLEDGMENT

To everyone who contributed to the realization of this project and kept me focus, thank you. My wife Dadria who insists on making sure the stories are at their best through the eyes of a woman point of views. My son Brian who inspired this whole undertaking. My parents Joseph and Yvona who are my keepers to whom acquired my being humble. The entire Alexanders family for putting up with me all these years. Last and not least, Robinson my one and only best friend.

I am forever indebted and grateful!

To God be the glory

INTRO

This is a familiar but timeless story of a man who worked his way up the ladder to seemingly have it all -- a loving wife, a lucrative position as a business entrepreneur, bountiful fortune, three finely raised children, and all the comforts and luxuries for a wonderful life. Yet, this very man had aberrant tendencies that would lead his marriage down rocky and murky pathways of lies, lust, kinky sex, deceptions, and betrayal!

Yes, this is all too common amongst us, and yet, there is something distinctive in this particular life story. Read on and you will see how the turn of events impacts on the man's stoic and steadfast wife – how the cycle of unrequited emotional love, depression, anxiety, and desperation ferments in the young lady's psyche and eventually overpowers her despite her best efforts. The final turn of events reveals the true essence of this story.

CAST OF CHARACTERS

Primary characters: Tim and Laurie

Children: Taylor, Ronny and Jade

Jenny: The other woman

Dexter: Friend/business partner, the
    instigator who influences.

A relationship is like a fledgling plant that sprouts from a seed. When nurtured with love and tender care, the plant gains strength and stature. Eventually it blossoms into a magnificent tree standing tall and strong through the ages, withstanding all the mighty forces of nature.

CHAPTER 1
THE JOURNEY

This is the story of Tim Mackintosh, a prominent businessman of Rockland County Florida with a wife, Laurie, and three kids, Taylor, Ronny, and Jade. His aspirations took him away from his hometown, Tuscan Creek Mississippi, and his folks who wanted him to stay to run a family-owned shop.

Early on, Tim's father had inherited a rich and luscious green acre of land. He decided to farm and raise cattle and sheep there and then open a family shop selling dairy products and vegetables. Tim was to inherit the shop, keep it running and keep the family legacy going. But that was not to be. Tim's fascination was with books and the bright big city lights. He was not going to be just a rural colored farm boy. He cast his eyes on bigger things, much bigger.

Tim was also a good football player at school. It became his passion to master the art of the game. Although he was exposed to the nitty-gritty of running a family business through his father, the idea did not entice him. When he received a full scholarship to play football at State Miami University (SMU), it was just what he wanted. He left for Florida without a second thought. His father was broken-hearted.

Tim made quite an impression in college. He was book savvy, ranked at the top of his class, and his good looks on top of all that was especially appealing to the ladies. One classmate in particular, Laurie, was drawn to his wealth of knowledge and seemingly humble appeal. Tim too had his eyes on Laurie but he did not yet let her know his interest.

Laurie did not move with his circle of "hip" buddies and their parties. She was conservative and rather reserved, certainly not a Prima Dona. Tim, meanwhile, was "living it up" with his gals in the dormitories in the weekends. What a transformation from a small town youngster from Mississippi to a mover and a shaker, speeding up the "fast lane!"

And then it happened, a significant shift in his demeanor. Everyone noticed. Tim was no more active in class discussions. Too tired, perhaps? He did spend the entire class session napping on and off the books. But still, he was excelling in each of the courses. How could he party throughout the weekend and turn in his assignments the next day? May be he's a fast learner, a brain super power, a genius?

Yes indeed, Tim had the makings of a genius, but not of the usual natural sort.

There was something else that boosted his energy like a fast moving train that later crashes. Laurie felt concern for dear Tim and decided to investigate the matter.

She approached him as he had his head down on his books after a class period. "I am alright"! He spluttered as Laurie offered to help him. She insisted on getting him a drink of water. He relented. His speech was largely incoherent. Noticing that he was in no condition to stand up, let alone drive his car back home, she grabbed his bag to search for his phone to call someone. She noticed in his bag two small bottles --- an antidepressant and another labeled "speed." Why would such a bright person be messing up with these horrible drugs? She thought to herself, in shock and disbelief.

Driven by a protective instinct, she confiscated the deadly pills and left him an apology note for "destroying his medical supplies". She then hailed a cab to take him home and found someone to drive his car back as well.

When Tim finally recovered from under the spell the next day, he had no recollection of the incident, except to feel a little woozy. After a long bath, he was back again to his usual scheme. But there were no antidepressants to be found in his backpack and the "speed" pills were missing. Searching through his bag, he found a note with the initial L.N (Laurie Knowles) addressed to him.

It was bizarre. He didn't understand how the note got inside his backpack. As he read through the note, he was moved by the message. Someone actually cared for his well-being. But who was this mystery person? During a class presentation, Laurie spoke about empathy -- how one act of kindness for another can change the world.

Tim quickly connected the dots -- the tone and tenor of her presentation was markedly like the message. The affirmation was more decisive when Laurie, walking behind him murmured, "Welcome Back!" Startled by the comment and the revelation, Tim turned around to face Laurie and smiled with a sigh of relief. He felt that he could trust her to keep the matter confidential. He did not want the secret to be exposed to the entire school.

The two exchanged numbers and began to date shortly thereafter. Tim was happy again and back to his old self -- doing less partying and engaging more in the school programs. He credited his newfound attitude to Laurie. They were inseparable.

Tim soon graduated with a degree in Business Administration and started his own consulting firm. Laurie entered her final year in clinical medicine. And then it happened – the news that Tim's father had passed away.

It was a hard hit for Tim. He realized that he never got to reconcile the differences he had with his father. It dawned on him that his father's intent was based on love. Ever since Tim's mother passed away during child-birth, he had done his utmost to instill in his motherless boy a sense of purpose. As a colored man, he was especially mindful of the road blocks that potentially stood in the way of his boy living up to his full potential. Having gone through rough roads of discrimination in rural Mississippi, he was going to protect Tim as best as he could by setting him up with a family business in which he could be his own man.

The trip back to Mississippi for the funeral was a difficult one. Laurie, who was by then Tim's fiancé, had wanted to get to know the man who had meant so much to Tim. Everyone who had helped to raise Tim after his grandmother died was there to receive them with open arms. In a graceful somber ceremony, they put their elder to rest. A deep void engulfed Tim.

After selling everything he had inherited, Tim returned to

the sunshine State. Soon after, the couple married and both embarked on thriving careers.

Tim set his sight on real estate, buying liquidated property to fix and then reselling them for profit. He became very successful at it. He also made a number of investments here and there, trading stocks on Wall Street. They could now afford a more lavish life style, a lot different from their humble beginnings. Laurie became a nurse at a local hospital. They purchased a yacht and went sailing whenever they could.

With this newfound happiness, Laurie thought she was living her dream – a perfect marriage, a wealthy husband, and a good career. It was like a fairytale "happily ever after." Tim frequently traveled overseas on business trip. He tried to stay connected with his wife via video chatting to make up for his absences. But something was starting to bother Laurie and make her feel insecure.

Tim's focus seemed to shift to other women. He was constantly complimenting their wardrobes and looks. He seemed to overlook Laurie's beauty and sex appeal, even her very presence. Content in other ways to her newfound life, Laurie did not want to muddy the waters by confronting Tim with her frustrations.

CHAPTER 2
A NEW BEGINNING

Things were about to get better for Laurie, career-wise. She was promoted to work as head nurse besides the cardio heart doctor in E.R. She welcomed the news with great pride, but she felt let down that Tim was not there to celebrate the big accomplishment with her. He was in Japan overseeing operation on an upcoming project. As Tim committed more and more long hours, days, and went to distant locations to his projects, the divide between them was growing wider.

They turned to Internet Chat Rooms for communication. But shortly thereafter, Tim was communicating very infrequently, even via Internet. He was too busy. Even phone calls were just every other day.

Nights were especially long for Laurie when Tim was away on business. She longed for his soft touch and caresses. She want only turned to pampering herself with sex objects. Masturbation fulfilled her needs and comforted her throughout the long night hours. Picturing his happy face when he returned home from trips was another way she sought relief.

Sensing the growing tensions between them, Tim tried to

resolve the problem. He was going to surprise his wife with an early return from one of his trips abroad. But Laurie had already left for work. She had taken the night shift just so that she didn't have to stay home lonely. When she returned home the next morning, it was a magical moment to be surprised by Tim. She melted into his arms and could not stop crying.

They rejoiced over a warm bath and a hot meal and savored every moment. In the two years of their relationship, she had never felt happier. With Tim at home, everything seemed right. She requested a leave of absence from her job to spent time with her husband. Weeks later, she received the great news -- she was expecting. Tim was thrilled. He was going to be a dad!

But the celebration was short lived as Tim prepared to board a flight back to Asia. The first trimester was especially hard for Laurie. Without Tim the pressure was mounting -- nobody to lean on. Laurie turned to some of her co-workers, one in particular, Jenny, who had developed a special bond with Laurie. She was a young inexperienced nurse in the intensive care unit.

They shared their passion for what they did. Jenny valued Laurie's knowledge and experience. Laurie was her role model. So it was quite natural for Laurie to turn to her loyal friend for emotional support. Jenny was her mainstay in critical moments throughout her pregnancy. Although Tim came home as often as he could, shortening his trips abroad to be by her side, it was Jenny who was with her at one of Laurie's most exciting moments yet – when the sonograph pictures of the unborn child were taken.

Tim was grateful to Jenny for all she was doing for Laurie and was ready to compensate her. But Jenny would have none of it. So Tim got her a car as a token of his appreciation.

Flattered by his generosity, Jenny became very fond of Tim. Likewise, Laurie and Tim regarded Jenny as a true, kind, and unselfish friend.

Months later, Laurie gave birth to a beautiful girl named Taylor. The void in Laurie's life was now seemingly filled with a blessing from heaven. Tim and Laurie grew closer. They perceived their new-born as a promise of great things to come. The Mackintoshes left the hospital to celebrate life and a new beginning with family and colleagues.

The cheer and excitement of the baby's coming settled down quickly as the reality of sleepless nights and constant cries took over. Laurie was an attentive mother, rushing to meet every need. Tim did little to help, sleeping through the nightly disturbances and taking a nonchalant laid back attitude in general.

The juggling act of balancing motherhood, job, and household matters tested Laurie's sanity. It was especially disturbing knowing that Tim was spending more and more time locked up in his office. Laurie's predicament was appeased, however, when Tim employed assistants to tackle everyday tasks around the house.

Tim found time for Baby Taylor, however. He was a proud father who loved to play that distinctive role with affection and bravado. Watching this enthusiasm, Laurie wondered at how this same man would turn a blind eye to her needs and look the other way when she needed help. Yet she loved seeing the two spend time together. The rest of it, she decided, had to do with the stress and demands of his career.

19

CHAPTER 3

FULL HOUSE

Laurie cherished her time with Taylor. She was growing up beautifully. At age one and a half, Laurie decided that it was time for her to return to her career, her passion for helping to care for the sick. Meanwhile, Tim's ventures overseas were growing remarkably successful. But success brought on increasing competition with other rivals. Tim gained the reputation of being a bombastic, harsh, and manipulative competitor. Laurie continued to support and defend Tim against his biggest critics.

Even at his low's, Laurie stood by Tim and helped to pull him through the hurdles. Growing increasingly self-centered, Tim hardly noticed Laurie's gentleness or the ingenious ways she protected him. Laurie was not shaken. She believed in their potential as a couple. She was unwavering and strong in her belief that a strong foundation equates to a good marriage. She was going to remain that strong foundation for their marriage and a devoted mother. When Taylor turned four, Laurie found herself pregnant again. Little Taylor was five at the time, starting to attend a privately run pre-school.

Tim was a good provider. He tried to be attentive but more as an after thought, something he must do after his needs were met, and not out of true compassion or empathy. He was particularly clueless of Laurie's emotional needs, especially in the critical months that led to the birth of Ronny.

Tim's apathetic nature was arguably in part a result of not having had a bonding relationship with his mother whom he had lost. And clearly, he did not bond very well with his father whose vision of life he did not share. He had a practical mind, however. As Laurie's emotional needs became more pressing and as she sought to gain attention and more understanding from him as the birthing date got closer, Tim's solution was to convince Laurie to take an early retirement to focus on motherhood.

Laurie gave birth to a handsome baby boy, whom they named Ronny. Laurie took meticulous care of the little ones from very early on. The helpers they hired were primarily for the upkeep of the house and for attending to household matters. Laurie took sole charge of the children. In her mind, they were too precious to be left to others. Her vision was having a big family whom she can individually mold and shape to do and be the best in life. Soon, little Ronny too was crawling and learning to walk like his big sister. And Taylor did a phenomenal job at teaching him the ropes. The two became inseparable.

Laurie's relationship with Tim, however, continued to be stressful. Her non-confrontational persona and her faith-based belief directed her toward tolerance and stoic acceptance in most matters. But she was taken by surprise each time a side of his personality emerged that seemed bizarre – his need to practice kinky sex that was not exactly to her liking. But as a dutiful wife, she weathered these developments in order to satisfy his sexual appetite.

Tim achievements skyrocketed in the ensuing years. The children were now adolescents. After years of building an empire abroad, he was now ready to branch it with the U.S. market. He relegated control over part of his company's assets to his most trusted advisor Dexter and named him the Chief Executor to manage things on the global scale.

Just as he was transitioning to move, the global market took a slump and was hit with one of the worst economic meltdowns. A new era had ushered in. Though the devastation had a great impact all around, the aftermath didn't affect the Asian's markets as much. But it did slow down production and demand. So, Tim returned to the States to be with the family. During the course of his stay, he was quite involved with the children and put together family getaways.

Everything seems to be going exceptionally well. However, the Mackintoshes were never alone in their field trips sailing the waves of the blue sea. They often had a special guest on board, Jenny. It was Tim's idea that she came along for the ride and Laurie agreed. Since she was a family friend, there was nothing that concerned her about his request. Tim also brought along his closest friend Dexter for the eight-day summer adventure.

There was clearly chemistry between Tim and Jenny. They shared the same love for the finest wines and even their zodiac signs matched. Through most of the trip, Jenny's eyes were admiring Tim's interactions with his wife. She envied their relationship. She went so far as to grab his attention with her flirtatious maneuvers and with attentive details that were more condescending than sincere. Laurie was too busy conversing with Dexter that she didn't notice her friend's sluttish behavior.

Tim's voracious sexual needs and Jenny's irresistible charm awakened in Tim his latent lustful desires. He manifested his needs like a sexual deviant on Laurie, bursting upon her ever so often that she took it to mean that he found her beautiful, as he once did, and was proving his love for her. She felt worthy in his presence. His fetish tendencies were becoming unquenchable. Laurie conceived her third child, the last of their offsprings. They named her Jade.

CHAPTER 4

DISCONNECTED

After years of dedication and hard work, juggling a career, and raising three kids, Laurie was ready to throw in the towel and focus on herself for a change. She started by revisiting that special place where it all started -- that first date which ignited the spark of a long lasting memory. Echoes of Tim's voice whispering sweet love in a clever poetic style resonated in the walls of her mind. Walking along the narrow path of the creek, she reminisced about their time together, romantically holding hands, and promising to uphold their vows faithfully.

She longed to recapture those moments with Tim, but his romantic flame seemed to have long since dwindled. Perhaps she should be less accepting of the situation, more upfront about her turmoil, and renew her commitment to him about making their relationship stronger, she thought. She anticipated his arms comforting her with eagerness as she opened up to him all her passions, fears, and frustrations. He would be more responsive if he knew her side of things, she reasoned.

For a while, Tim seemed to hear Laurie's concerns loud and clear. He responded with a genuine assurance that he would try to make a change for the better. He was going to make up for letting her believe, through his neglect, that she was unattractive, especially after the birth of their third child.

In the early years of their marriage, pampering was the staple of their love affair. Tim's signature move was to surprise the Mrs. in memorable ways -- From breakfast in bed every morning to a foot rub massage in the evening. One of the things that really made her smile was when Tim turned on her favorite contemporary jazz music at the start of the day. His spontaneity and creative humor were boundless. Once he had her tour around the city in a helicopter to capture a beautiful view.

There used to be nothing too big for Tim's imagination. He would throw extravagant parties to show Laurie off to the world and publicly pronounce his love for her. Within their circles, they were seen as powerful couples to be modeled after. They were constantly holding hands like high school sweethearts.

Tim was like a courtier in the early years of their marriage, proving that chivalry wasn't dead. Little efforts like opening the doors and pulling out seats at regular venues went a long way for Laurie to feel special. Their sexual intimacy used to be just as profound and consistent. Now Tim seemed to be embroiled in a world entirely of his own. Laurie took it to heart that he was prone to forget her birthday, the birthday bash he had traditionally held each year, and even their wedding anniversary.

To his credit, Tim tried to make up for his shortcomings. He gave Laurie access to his accounts and encouraged her to splurge on designer wear and whatever other special gifts she chose to buy.

CHAPTER 5

BAD INFLUENCE

Tim's wealth served not only as an appeasement for Laurie, he was going to go full blast with it. He started on a new hobby with Dexter – frequenting strip clubs every other weekend. Dexter who was a frequent traveler to the brothels of Bangkok planted the idea of pursuing sexual fantasies through a wide variety of ways. Dexter lauded the pleasures of observing women degrade themselves through nudity and kinky acts. Dexter, clearly a misogynist and an arrogant one at that, was not well regarded by people in general. But to Tim, Dexter was his alter ego. Yearnings for lust and licentious living was growing ever more pervasive in Tim's mind with each passing day and Dexter's adventures served to justify those yearnings. Morality issues did not matter. It was as if they thought themselves God's gift to women.

Laurie interestingly went along with Tim's newfound pleasure, particularly since he seemed to be upfront about his needs and was unapologetic about them. She was even drawn into his line of argument that it was an exotic trend for men to go to strip joints. She felt that his new inclinations would spice up their relationship even more.

Indeed, it seemed to work. Tim's sexual confidence and savagery in the bedroom after each of his visits to the strip club peaked Laurie's interest and excitement. Tim was ready for more excitement. He marveled at how Dexter was like a local celebrity in the strip clubs, with women flocking to his arms even as he entered the joints. It was what he wanted too. With plenty of wealth to go around, money was not an issue.

Pretty soon, Tim's popularity skyrocketed to a new height in the street circles while Dexter had to pare down his escapades. With his company having to cut back its budget due to economic slump, private jets were no longer available. Tim, on the other hand, was on a climb for even more excitement. Saturday nights, Tim was a regular at the Bugaboo nightclub tipping singles on strippers in the G-string, swiping the poll, and entertaining their cheek bun to the groove sounds.

With his proven confidence and name recognition, Tim no longer needed to tailgate behind Dexter or be blessed by his seal of approval. His fascination with the dancers was by now getting too close for comfort for Laurie. One night, Tim accidentally slipped another woman's name – Peaches – during a role-playing of kinky sex with Laurie. Even his dreams couldn't escape the memorable seductive soirees at the Bugaboo.

The nights were becoming increasingly unpleasant for Laurie. She was flabbergasted by the nature of the kinky sex and could not reconcile any more to Tim living out his fantasies vicariously through her. She suspected that he was in this binge not for the sake of strengthening their relationship but for the sheer interest of imaginarily cavorting with other women. When she confronted him with this revelation, he went on the attack. After all, she had been in full agreement with him on the arrangement from the start. He blamed Laurie for his choice of leisure, arguing that she had benefited from it.

The downward slide in their relationship was all but inevitable. Laurie accused Tim of infidelity and argued that his activities were bringing dishonor to their marriage. Tim's line of defense was that Laurie was exaggerating. He continued to party without any show of remorse.

Laurie's ordeal was reaching a crescendo. She could no longer contain her anguish. She had to seek help. So she turned to the one person who had befriended her in the past – Jenny. Tim didn't want to be outdone, so he contacted Dexter to get his take on the way things had developed. Dexter, as expected, flatly remarked, "Where there's no truce love doesn't exist." How and where he came up with the slogan is unclear but he was giving ammunition to Tim's stance that Laurie was in the wrong for doubting Tim's love for her and for believing that he was unfaithful to her in body and spirit.

From then on, Tim acted like an emotionally outraged victim. He begrudged his wife for her stance and misinterpreted her frustrations as a sign of controlling.

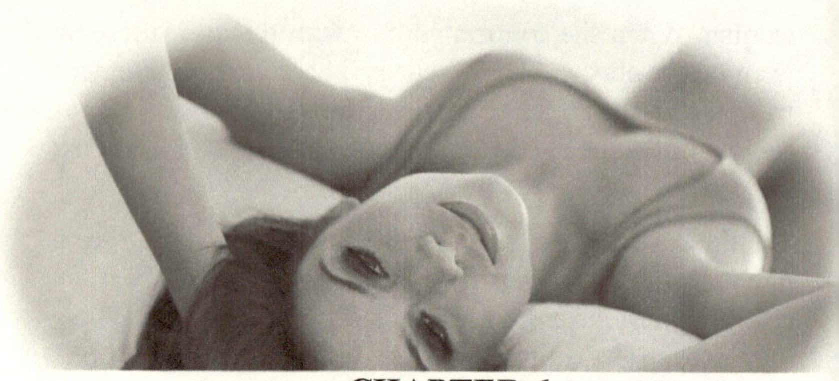

CHAPTER 6
EXOTIC TREND

The "exotic" trend into which Tim was now full immersed knew no bounds. His imagination was in full swing into the world of curvature waists and voluptuous booties. His wife's round bottom was of average size, he noted. He was now obsessed with more fulsome, bouncy derrieres and sexy gaits. Since his wife was already accusatory, he took it upon himself to feel no qualms about breaking his fidelity vows in every possible way.

His misogynistic tendencies and lure comments about women's bodies became a constant in Laurie's company, around relatives, and in the least likely places like family gatherings. At the same time, his arduous yearnings for certain female movie stars made him increasingly critical of Laurie's looks. This extreme combination of deprecation of ordinary women and hero worship of others made Laurie very insecure about her looks, and her very identity. Was she beautiful enough for him? Can she live up to his expectations? To make matters worse, Tim would jokingly remark that he would consider marrying one of her distant cousins as a replacement for Laurie in the event that something happens.

Tim's remarks grew increasingly distasteful over time and he would mock Laurie in public, revealing and shocking everyone with the flaws in their relationship. As money became more abundant, his ego was ballooning. His wealth made him feel powerful and all knowing. He was entitled to his opinions and his words (including some absurd insinuations) deserved to be applauded, he thought. Of course, Laurie was flabbergasted and overcome with grief by his transformation. Oftentimes, she would storm out of the room with tears and embarrassment. Yet, her loyalty and above all, her love for her children silenced her. At all cost, Laurie was going to avoid conflict with her husband for the sake of the children.

In a quiet, firm and resolute way, however, Laurie sought to appeal to Tim's senses. In private moments, she reasoned with him about his disrespectful tone and about him regaining his self-discipline. But there was no letting up – only resistance, denial, and worse, more demeaning remarks. Laurie chose to believe even then that Tim will outgrow this stage, that it was all a matter of misunderstanding. At worse, the change in his personality, she hoped, would not cause him irrevocable harm in the business world in which he moved.

Letting go, unfortunately, proved to be a mistake. Laurie was in for a surprise development that would cost her dearly.

CHAPTER 7
BETRAYAL

When there is confusion and heartache, having a close friend to turn to would naturally be the comforting thing to do. Jenny became that confidante to Tim and Laurie. Unfortunately for Laurie, Jenny proved to be an opportunist whose intentions were anything but noble. She had her eye on Tim ever since the early days when he generously gave her a car for the kindness she had shown Laurie. His growing fortunes made him even more enticing.

Pretending to be their problem-solver, Jenny offered them a sympathetic ear. Stealthily, however, she befriended Tim over Laurie, letting him know that Laurie was entirely to blame for their problems. Tim was surprised by Jenny's turnover. He was heartened, however, that Laurie's closest friend understood his situation.

It was not long before an unbreakable bond developed between Tim and Jenny that Laurie did not see coming. Jenny was a regular in their household, playing both sides, deliberately attempting to sabotage the marriage. Intrigued by Jenny's seeming "genuineness," Tim was developing strong feelings toward her. She further enticed him through her sexy outfits and seductive body language.

Not long thereafter, Tim invited Jenny to his penthouse where he expressed his feelings over the sky-rise balcony.

The romance between Jenny and Tim flourished even while Tim frequented the strip joints. Initially it was secret passionate exchanges over the phone. Then Tim proposed that she dance for him as exotic dancers do. Jenny was flattered. Soon after the two of them met at a Four Season's hotel and spent a heated night of passion. The romance lasted four months.

Laurie unsuspectingly came upon them in a compromising position in a public venue. Stunned and feeling betrayed, Laurie kept after them through a private detective and caught them cavorting in a hotel room. Tim showed no remorse. Instead he blamed Laurie for his need for other women. Meanwhile Jenny took off, running from embarrassment. She disappeared from sight. That evening Laurie's world came tumbling down.

CHAPTER 8
CONFLICTED

Laurie realized that all her compromises over the years had yielded nothing but misery. Everything she had hoped for and strived to build lay in ruin. The person she trusted the most and shared her utmost intimate feelings had deceived her through the years and now betrayed her with her best friend. She was confused and unable to accept the extent of their affair -- that it happened under her very nose. Their seemingly casual interactions were anything but, she realized. Although she was aware of her husband's shenanigans in the world of exotic women, she didn't think he had it in him to lay on her this final brutality and to then take no responsibility for it. Could this be the same Tim she married, the chivalrous, doting husband and loving father to their children?

Once again, Laurie attributed Tim's failings and those of their marriage to herself. Somehow she had failed him as a wife, as he had the habit of accusing her, and denied her children the possibility of a happy home.

Their vow of "death do us apart" that she had valued had become obviated and meaningless with each passing day.

For the sake of the children, however, Tim and Laurie created a facade of normalcy and fictitious admiration for each other. They would gather at the dinner table as a family with fake composure. At one occasion, Laurie was unable to swallow down the food. Young Jade noticing that something was amiss asked Laurie, "Are you ok Mommy?" Laurie quickly excused herself and ran to her room upstairs and burst into tears. Tim had to explain to the children that their mother was going through stress.

Every night, as time went on, they waited until every one of the kids was asleep to break apart into different rooms. Laurie would get the bedroom and Tim slept in the pent house next door. Their cover-up went on for months.

One night, Laurie had a vivid nightmare, an illusory flashback of their first meeting. In her dream she was drugged and trapped in a dark alley surrounded by a thick glass wall that was overflowing with water. More such nightmares started to engulf her nights. Laurie fought and wrestled with her demons, shouting in distress, "No, no, no!" In each such instance, she was at some treacherous place, powerless and in despair, while her children were being taking away from her. She would often wake up in shock and despair as the dreams reached their climax. At one such occasion, she got up and went to the bathroom to wet her face with a damp cloth. She then went to the living room, wrapped herself in a blanket and sank into her sofa. Ronny, her second son woke up at about the same time to pee and then went on to the kitchen through the living room for a glass of milk.

At first, he didn't notice the tucked up roll on the couch since there was little lighting. But, as he walked past, he heard muffled sobs coming from nearby. Not knowing who or what it was, he called out fearfully, "Who is there"? The crying got louder and Ronny quickly turned on the light to find his mother crawled up on the sofa. "What's wrong Ma"? he inquired worriedly, holding her tightly in his arms. Laurie tried to lighten the matter by attributing the incident to a quarrel she just had with Tim. But Ronny was not convinced. He tenaciously demanded answers. Adamant about protecting her children her sufferings, she simply stated that the truth will come out soon but that there was nothing to fear since they were a solid family who would always be together no matter what.

Meanwhile, Ronny confided in the only person he could trust, his older sister Taylor. But Taylor had a hard time believing Ronny because their mother seemed happy from all that she had observed. Ronny set out to disprove his sister by taking her down one night to where their mother lay sobbing.

Once again, Laurie assured them it'll be alright. Determined to get to the truth, the children persisted with their inquiries, insisting that they were old enough to understand. Indeed, they were in their teens, two years apart from each other, and going to high school. Laurie finally gave in. Their father, she said, had an extra marital affair with her closest friend. They were seeking counseling to resolve their irreconcilable differences. Taylor and Ronny promised not to disclose the information to Jade who was then just 6 years old.

The counseling sessions were in part productive. Both of them let out their feelings and sentiments, disagreed with each other, argued their positions forcefully, and ultimately, through professional intervention, came to a fuller understanding of each other and their own missteps. Laurie conceded that she was in part to blame for encouraging his lifestyle, but it also became clear from Tim's admission that his sexual habits first developed overseas. Starting as a mild sexual fantasy, the instinct mushroomed into a bestial addiction that ultimately led to infidelity. Tim disclosed that he loved his wife and vowed to fix the damages he had caused.

CHAPTER 9
EXIT WOUND

Marriage counseling did not quite heal Laurie's wounds. Hopelessness had descended upon her despite all that Tim tried to say and do to make amends. She saw through it all. Tim was never going to be the man she had envisioned him to be all her life. Even when she had ample opportunities to see him for what he really was, she had not seen.

This time around, the lavish family vacations and expensive gifts that used to palliate her, no longer had the same effect. The scars of the betrayal and the resulting scandal had left indelible marks on her psyche.

Laurie was more detached than ever. Her eyes were expressionless with no focus, and her spirit was drifting to dark and isolated corners. For months at a time she was haunted by demons through her nightmares. She sought safety by isolating herself from people.

Laurie was diagnosed as suffering from clinical depression and social anxiety disorder. The problem got so severe that Tim's every move sparked tension and accusations. Without Tim's knowledge, Laurie was having Tim's telephone conversations monitored to further ascertain to herself that he was going to be a repeat offender.

Laurie had lost faith and trust in Tim. She was sure that he would get back to his old habits regardless of how forcefully he had pleaded otherwise. Their romance was long gone and all she felt was the indignity of it all.

To relieve the misery of a fruitless existence and a past that was irreconcilable, she started to inflict physical injuries on herself. She gained morbid pleasure, for instance, on cutting her wrists. That was one of her ways to cope with mental anguish.

Watching kinship and unity among other couple brought on pangs of envy and a sense a great loss. "How did it go so wrong?" Laurie wondered. One moment she was living the dream of a perfect marriage. In the next, she was fighting to keep afloat that foundation only to find herself slipping to a ravine. Tim's efforts to fix the debacle did not seem genuine to her. His motivation, she reasoned, is pity for her. Her self-preservations was from keeping more distance from him.

In her heart of hearts, Laurie longed for what she knew she would never have – the man she had envisioned all her life, one who would love, respect, admire, and cherish her, and hold her in this darkest hour to comfort her.

Laurie's long battle with depression was taking its toll. Her moods swings were becoming more and more erratic. In a surprise birthday party that Tim held for Laurie with guests including her favorite past colleagues (with the exception of Jenny of course) and family, Laurie suddenly lost control, switching minute by minute from laughter to crying, from quiet and smiling demeanor to an angry and heated woman with furious outbursts. The children rallied to the support of their mother, but Laurie was even retreating from them.

Within months, Laurie was becoming her only true trusted adviser. She guarded herself from everyone else.

CHAPTER 10
THE EULOGY

In the ensuing months, Tim resumed his secret alliance with Jenny. It should have come as no surprise to him, therefore, that she called to tell him that she might be pregnant with his child since her menstrual periods had stopped.

The news of her alleged expectancy was a source of great consternation for Tim. He denied that it was his child she was carrying and accused her of extortion.

Feeling abandoned and insulted by Tim's refusal to accept the outcome of her situation, Jenny was ready to wreak her vengeance. She was especially outraged that Tim had promised her the world and a life together. Jenny was not going to let him off the hook that easily. Secretly, she arranged a meeting with Laurie at an outside cafe eatery. She disclosed to Laurie that she was intimate with her husband and that she was pregnant with his baby.

It took all of Laurie's mental energy to restrain herself from seizing the woman by her throat and chocking the hell out of her. The battle she fought inwardly was quite remarkable for someone with severe depression and fierce animosity, but after a few brief minutes of taking in the information, she managed to put on the appearance of quiet composure. She congratulated Jenny and merely said, "I hope it was all worth it."

In the weeks that followed, the two exchanged bitter words and parted company.

After months of alienation, Laurie finally faced Tim with the newest revelation. In a firm and resolute voice she factually laid out the details of her agonies and stresses -- all that he had put her under throughout their marriage. Tim was reduced to cowering under her forceful attack.

Afterwards, Laurie moved around in a decisive way, as if to clear up matters before a long journey. She attended to her children's needs lovingly. On a clear spring morning, while everyone was away, she wrote her will and testament. She had special words of love, wisdom and admiration for her children, telling them she counted on them to always look after each other. She thanked Tim for giving her three wonderful children and asked him to make sure he doesn't miss the mark the next time around.

There was nothing more left to do, nothing more she wanted from life, nothing more that would ease the pain of a broken heart. Laurie drove to the busy bridge of interstate ninety-eight that very day. She walked out of the car bare footed, hopped on the suspender bars and jumped to her death.

Tim was at a meeting with a potential client when he heard the news of Laurie's untimely death of an apparent suicide. Overcome with shock and grief, he rushed to the E.R. and found the lifeless body of his wife.

The funeral was largely arranged by the children with the help of family. While Tim took care of the expenses, the family limited his participation in the services. At the very end, however, he was given the chance to pay his final respects and give the eulogy. As he stood up on the church podium next to the casket to say his peace, a sudden brush of air glazed his face and he poignantly looked upward to recapture a final vision of their happy days.

TO BE CONTINUED......

STORY CONTINUES IN PART II

ABOUT THE AUTHOR

Gregy Alexander is a Writer and a Storyteller. He started to write his novels in different types of genre to escape the pain from his reality and found solace in writing everything from erotica romance novels to poetry and children books. Four years ago, he published his first novel under the pseudonym Jean Alexander. In his tell tale stories, enter the mind of a conscientious fragile visionary.

www.ingramcontent.com/pod-product-compliance
Lightning Source LLC
Chambersburg PA
CBHW020624120726
47905CB00003B/926